The Secret of the Wooden Chest

15% of the profits from the sale of this book will
be donated to BBC Children in Need,
registered charity number 802052.

The Secret of the Wooden Chest

A Roman Magic book
BOOK ONE

Catherine Rosevear

Front cover illustration and logo by
Ian R. Ward

Matador
9 Priory Business Park,
Wistow Road, Kibworth Beauchamp,
Leicestershire. LE8 0RX
Tel: 0116 279 2299
Email: books@troubador.co.uk
Web: www.troubador.co.uk/matador
Twitter: @matadorbooks

ISBN 978 1788032 537

British Library Cataloguing in Publication Data.
A catalogue record for this book is available from the British Library.

Printed and bound in the UK by TJ International, Padstow, Cornwall
Typeset in 11pt Baskerville by Troubador Publishing Ltd, Leicester, UK

Matador is an imprint of Troubador Publishing Ltd

For Michael and Emma

To find out more about Roman Magic books,
and for information about further books in the series
featuring Hannah and Mrs Oberto,
follow Catherine Rosevear on
@cathrosevear on Twitter,
@CatherineRosevear2 on Facebook,
or visit www.catherinerosevear.wordpress.com

Chapter 1

A loud slamming noise woke Hannah with a start. She lay still for a few moments, rubbing her eyes, before lifting her head from the pillow and peering around her shadowy bedroom. A faint gleam of light showed beneath the curtains. It must be nearly dawn. What could have woken her? It had sounded like the front door, but that was an unusual noise to hear in the middle of the night. Whatever could have happened?

Propping herself up on her pillow, Hannah remembered that the office phone had rung just as she was getting ready for bed the previous evening, and Mum had run to answer it. Hannah's mum always seemed to be rushing about, as she worked as the Matron in charge of a nursing home. The nursing home took up most of the building, but Hannah and her parents lived in a small flat on the top floor.

Mum had said something over the phone about 'whatever time you arrive will be fine'. Presumably someone wanted to arrange to look around the nursing home the next day, to see if they'd like to move in. Most of the people in the home were very old and had been living there for many years, but there was one room available. Maybe the late phone call and now the slamming of the front door meant that someone was moving in as an emergency case? This had happened once before, when old Mr Herbert had arrived. He'd moved into the nursing home when his sister had become too ill to look after him, planning to stay only until she was better, but he'd enjoyed it more than he'd expected. Three years later, he was still living with them and chatting cheerfully to Hannah's dad every day about football.

Hannah pushed her long brown hair back from her face and peered through the half-light, screwing up her eyes to check the time. Nearly five o'clock. If a new person was moving into the nursing home's empty room, it was unlikely she'd meet him or her until after school. She decided not to worry about it for now. Closing her eyes, she lay back down, pulled the covers up to her chin and slowly drifted back to sleep.

By the time she got up for breakfast, Mum was already busy at work downstairs in the nursing home, but Dad was in the kitchen of their top-floor flat, wearing his tattered, paint-spattered overalls.

'What was happening last night, Dad?' Hannah asked, yawning, as she squeezed between the wall and the table, and pulled out a battered kitchen chair. The disturbed night had left her more tired than she'd expected.

'A new lady moved in as an emergency.' Dad looked in the cupboard for a cup that wasn't chipped. 'Her house burnt down yesterday evening, but the firemen managed to get her out okay. Not many of her possessions have been saved, though. She's got some clothes with her, but that's about it.' He poured Hannah some orange juice, spilling some onto his already dirty overalls in the process, and slopping quite a bit onto the wobbly kitchen table.

'How awful for her,' Hannah said thoughtfully, absentmindedly wiping up the mess Dad had made before helping herself to some cornflakes. 'Is she alright?'

'It's hard to say.' Dad passed Hannah the milk. 'I didn't see much of her. Your mum was settling her in, but I don't think the new lady said much. I think she might be Italian.' He put his coffee cup in the sink and bent down to check his reflection in the glass door of the oven. 'I must get a haircut soon. Not today though. I've got to fix the radiator on the landing before I can even make a start on putting up Mr Wilson's new curtains.'

Dad did all the practical work around the nursing home, and he could turn his hand to almost anything. Plumbing, carpentry, decorating and gardening were all in his line of work. 'Anything but electrics,' he often said cheerfully, when Mum gave him his list of jobs.

Mum was always busy. She managed the assistant nurses, sorted out the medicines and did all the organising and office work. Because she was always working, it was Dad who made sure that Hannah was ready for school, and usually he had time for a chat with her in the mornings before she left. Hannah was completely different to both her parents. Her dad was great at practical jobs and her mum was good at medical things, but Hannah loved the social side of life and the chance to chat. She was an only child, and made up for the lack of a brother or sister by spending time with the people who lived downstairs. She spent hours talking to them, and hearing about the jobs they had done in their younger years, the lives they had led and the different things they were interested in.

Hannah finished her breakfast, picked up her school bag and then headed downstairs into the nursing home. As she went, she called goodbye to Dad, who was washing up the breakfast dishes. Passing the new lady's room, she glanced curiously at the firmly closed door. Not a sound. Maybe she was still asleep. Hannah was intrigued. Dad had said that this lady might be Italian, and she had never met an Italian person before. Would the new lady speak any English? If so, would she chat to Hannah sometimes, or perhaps even become her friend, like several of the other nursing home residents? Of course the new lady might not stay for long, but even so, Hannah couldn't wait to meet her.

Chapter 2

Before she left for school each morning, Hannah liked to pop into the residents' lounge and say hello to anyone who was there. She knew two of the assistant nurses who were in today quite well. Lizzie was friendly, and was always happy to have a chat with Hannah at break times. Joanne, the other assistant who was working that morning, was very different and sometimes could be quite rude. When Hannah peeked around the lounge door, she noticed Joanne was in there, tidying up yesterday's newspapers. Hannah frowned and decided to walk straight by. However, as she walked on, she heard a cry of 'Grub!' from the direction of a chair tucked away in a corner of the lounge.

It was so loud that Joanne jumped and dropped all the papers she had been picking up. 'Really, Mrs Beadle,' she exclaimed crossly. 'Did you have to do that?'

A tiny old lady, almost hidden by the sides of her enormous armchair, ignored Joanne and called out again, 'Come here, Grub.'

As Hannah walked into the lounge, she saw a little, white-haired old lady in a flowery skirt, smiling happily at her from the depths of a huge chair, her small feet several inches off the floor. Hannah smiled back warmly. She had known Mrs Beadle ever since she could remember. When Hannah was a toddler, she hadn't been able to pronounce 'Beadle' and so had always called this particular lady 'Mrs Beetle' instead. Mrs Beetle had loved this, and had immediately said that she would always call Hannah 'Grub', as a grub is a baby beetle.

Doll-like Mrs Beetle was over one hundred years old, but she showed no signs of getting ready to slow down. With her flowery clothes, curly white hair, bright smile and love of romantic novels, Mrs Beetle's personality seemed almost too big to fit inside her little body.

'Are you ready for school then, Grub?' Mrs Beetle demanded, pointedly smoothing her skirt and ignoring Joanne, who was trying to reach a newspaper that had fallen behind the chair. Hannah reached down for the paper and handed it to Joanne, who took it sullenly and stalked out of the lounge.

'I think so.' Hannah moved Mrs Beetle's library book so that she could sit down in the armchair next to her. 'I love your skirt, Mrs Beetle. Is that a new one?'

Mrs Beetle's wrinkled pink cheeks glowed with pleasure. 'You noticed,' she smiled, her dimples showing. 'Yes, it is new. I asked my daughter to get it for me when she took me out last week. As soon as I saw it, it reminded me straight away of the good old days.'

As a young woman, Mrs Beetle had spent several years as a professional ballroom dancer, and she loved to relive the highlights from this part of her life. She stared into the distance. 'I remember one night in – now, when would it be? Anyway, I was wearing the most beautiful ball gown. Pale rose silk with flowers embroidered all around the hem, it was. It swirled about so wonderfully when I danced. Not that I can dance like that these days, of course, but this skirt really reminded me of it.' Mrs Beetle fell silent as she stared into the distance, caught up in her memories. She sighed deeply, pulled herself back to the present with a shake of her head, and looked fondly at Hannah, before glancing at her more sharply. 'You look tired, Grub,' she observed. 'Didn't you sleep well?'

'Well, I am quite tired today,' admitted Hannah. 'I woke up when the new lady arrived in the night. Did you?'

'Oh yes,' said Mrs Beetle, who was always at the forefront of any gossip or news around the nursing home. 'When your mum helped me get dressed this morning, she told me that the poor lady's house had burnt down. Burnt right down to the ground as well. Nothing left, I heard.'

'That's awful, isn't it?' replied Hannah. 'I think I'll ask Mum if I can go in and say hello to her when I get back from school later. Dad said she might be Italian.' She frowned as a sudden thought struck her. 'I wonder if she's got any family in this country. It might be difficult for her, if not.'

Mrs Beetle nodded towards the lounge door. 'Don't worry, I'll soon show her the ropes. Anyway, you'd better get off now. I can hear your mum's medicine trolley rattling down the corridor, and she won't be pleased if she finds you still here.' This was true. Only the previous week Hannah had been chatting for too long to Mrs Beetle, and Mum had caught her and told her off for leaving late for school. That time it had been twenty to nine, but a quick glance at her watch now told Hannah that it was already ten to nine!

Hannah waited for the sound of the rattling medicine trolley to fade, as her mum entered a room further along the corridor, and then, after whispering a quiet goodbye to Mrs Beetle, she slipped out of the lounge. She grabbed her bag from where she'd left it in the hall and raced out of the building and down the drive. If she were lucky, she'd catch up with her best friend Lucy before she got to school.

Chapter 3

School seemed to last forever that day. There was still no word from the teacher about what the class's new topic was going to be that term, either. Hannah knew that it would be something historical, and as history was one of her favourite subjects, she was keen to know what they would be learning about. There was no news about this, though, and on top of that she wanted to get home quickly, to see if she would be allowed to meet the new Italian lady.

Finally half past three arrived, and Hannah called goodbye to Lucy before rushing away. Arriving home, she walked through the front door and straight away noticed a strange smoky smell. She sniffed and looked around curiously, until her eyes settled on a wooden chest that sat in the middle of the hall table. It certainly hadn't been there when she had left for school that morning. She walked closer to it, and as she did so the smoky smell got stronger. The chest looked quite old and battered, and seemed to be blackened around the edges. It was made of dark wood, and was fitted with a large fancy lock that looked as though it could be made of silver but needed a good clean.

Hannah sniffed cautiously as she approached the chest, but just as she was reaching out a hand towards it, Dad appeared round the corner of the stairs. 'Don't touch that, Hannah,' he called out, running down the last few steps. 'It's just arrived for the new lady, but I think it needs a good wipe down before anyone touches it. It's covered in soot.' He walked over to the table and looked down at the chest. 'The police brought it round just now. The firemen managed to rescue it from Mrs Oberto's house now the fire is properly out, but it's filthy. If you touch it you'll be spreading soot and mess all over the house.' He glared at the chest as if blaming it for causing so much trouble.

'Okay, Dad, don't worry, I won't touch it.' Hannah looked at the stairs behind Dad. She couldn't help noticing that, despite his concern for keeping things clean, he had left muddy boot prints all over the carpet. She smiled. 'Is "Mrs Oberto" the new lady's name?'

'That's right. She's Italian, I think, but she can speak quite good English. Seems pretty quiet so far, though, but of course she's had a stressful time.' Dad frowned to himself.

'Will I be allowed to say hello to her?'

'I don't know,' answered Dad. 'You'll have to ask your mum. I know you're always keen to suss out the new arrivals.'

Hannah smiled. He knew her so well. 'Did you manage to fix that radiator, Dad?'

'Pretty much, but lots of dirty water needing taking

out of it…' Dad's voice trailed off as his gaze followed Hannah's, first to his boots, and then the stair carpet behind him.

'Do you want a hand to clean the stairs, Dad?' Hannah offered, smiling.

Dad sighed. 'No. Thanks for offering though,' he mumbled. 'I'll go and get the cleaning bucket.'

Hannah went upstairs to the flat, dropped her school bag in her bedroom and then made her way back downstairs to the nursing home office. Mum could often be found there in the afternoons, and sure enough there she was, sitting at the desk.

She looked up with a tired smile when Hannah walked in. 'Hi, Hannah. I hope you've had a good day at school.' She seemed to already know what Hannah had come to ask. 'If you want to knock on Mrs Oberto's door, it's fine to go and say hello to her, so long as she says you can go in.' Mum turned back to her paperwork.

Hannah didn't need telling twice, and with a quick hug for Mum she was off down the corridor, narrowly avoiding bumping into Joanne and finally coming to a stop outside Mrs Oberto's door. Feeling excited at the prospect of meeting the new lady at last, she raised her hand and knocked loudly.

Chapter 4

There was a sudden shout from the other side of the door. Hannah couldn't be sure what it meant, but she decided to assume that she could go in. Turning the handle, she pushed the door open. She was surprised to find that the room was almost entirely dark, and for a while she couldn't make out anything at all in the gloom. As her eyes adjusted, she could see that the bedroom curtains were closed, and all the lights off.

'Come all the way in, do not stand about there!' bellowed a deep voice, in a strong foreign accent. Hannah jumped, and stepped forward. 'Who are you?' the voice demanded, from the direction of the bed. Hannah turned and saw the dim outline of a person dressed in black, lying on top of the bed covers.

'Hello,' she said nervously. 'I'm Hannah. I'm Matron's daughter and I live in the flat upstairs.' There was a harrumphing noise from the bed, but no other reply. 'I thought I'd come to say hello,' Hannah continued, hoping that Mrs Oberto wouldn't notice the nervousness in her voice. 'I'm very sorry to hear about your house fire. Would you like me to turn on the light for you?'

'If you wish to,' the voice croaked harshly. Hannah fumbled for the light switch. She blinked with surprise as the lights went on. There was a large lady lying back against the pillows, dressed entirely in black, and with a long woollen shawl draped around her head and shoulders, from the edges of which some unruly black hair peeped out. Her large, dark eyes watched Hannah suspiciously from beneath heavy eyebrows. In contrast to her plain black clothes, the lady wore a pink satin ribbon around her neck like a necklace, with a small silver key hanging from it.

Hannah tried to smile, but she found both the lady and her dark clothing so strange and unwelcoming that it was hard not to look surprised.

'Do not just stand there! Now you are here, you can get for me a cup of tea,' Mrs Oberto ordered, her thick eyebrows lowering into a frown.

'Yes, I will,' replied Hannah quickly, relieved to have a reason to leave. Bolting from the room, she hurried to the big kitchen on the ground floor, where all the residents' meals were prepared. As she waited for the kettle to boil, she wondered about the new lady she had just met. She wasn't sure that they would be friends after all and she felt a bit disappointed, not to say a little frightened, by this large, intimidating person with such a strange accent.

Should she just ask one of the assistant nurses to take the cup of tea to Mrs Oberto, so that she didn't have to go back into the new lady's room herself? She could just see Lizzie at the far end of the corridor. She felt sure that Lizzie wouldn't mind carrying the cup in for her. After thinking about it for a minute, though, Hannah decided this wouldn't be polite to Mrs Oberto. Squaring her shoulders, she got the tea ready and carried it nervously back towards Mrs Oberto's room. Perhaps she would just put down the cup and then make an excuse to leave again. However, when she got there, Dad was just carrying in the old wooden chest. He'd given it a good clean, and the smoky smell seemed to have almost gone.

'Here we go, Mrs Oberto,' said Dad. 'Hopefully everything inside will be fine.'

Hannah looked at Mrs Oberto to see if she would say anything in reply, but as the chest was laid gently down on the bedside table, Mrs Oberto's thin hand fluttered up to touch the silver key hanging from her neck, and her eyes filled with tears. Dad began to look uneasy, and muttering something about asking a nurse to pop in, he backed out of the room. He was never comfortable when someone he didn't know well started to cry, but Hannah reacted very differently. As she saw a tear roll down Mrs Oberto's cheek, her fear of this strange new lady melted away, and she felt full of sympathy. She walked over to the bed and sat down, laying her hand on Mrs Oberto's arm.

'Don't worry, Mrs Oberto, I'm sure everything will get sorted out,' she whispered.

Mrs Oberto sniffed loudly, and then unexpectedly felt for Hannah's hand and gave it a squeeze. 'Thank you, my dear,' she said, speaking much more softly than before. 'You should leave me now, so that I can see if the chest has kept my things safe.' Shakily, she took the pink ribbon from around her neck, and fitted the silver key into the lock of the chest before looking up at Hannah, suddenly seeming a little shy. 'But maybe you will come to see me again tomorrow?'

'Of course I will, Mrs Oberto,' said Hannah. She stood up to go, and gave Mrs Oberto a braver smile this time. 'Of course I will.'

Chapter 5

As the days passed, Mrs Oberto began to trust Hannah more, and the two of them spent a lot of time talking together. In her rich Italian accent, Mrs Oberto described to Hannah how the terrible fire at her house had started. It seemed that she had been in the habit of lighting a real fire in her living room fireplace, and had enjoyed sitting in front of it, even when the weather was quite warm. One day while Mrs Oberto was in the kitchen, cooking, the draught coming down the living room chimney had blown a spark from the fireplace onto the carpet, which had caught alight. The fire had spread quickly. If it hadn't been for a neighbour noticing the smoke coming from an open window, and calling the fire brigade, Mrs Oberto could easily have been killed. Because of this she was now afraid to have even the electric lights on in her room when she was alone, and preferred to sit in the dark when no one was with her.

Mrs Oberto also told Hannah more about her early life. She was quick to say that she was not from the Italian mainland at all, but was in fact from Sicily, a large sunny island near the southern end of Italy. She explained that, although Sicily belonged to Italy and the people there spoke Italian, the Sicilians remained fiercely protective of their own identity and customs. Mrs Oberto told Hannah about how she had had a wonderful childhood in the golden sunshine and pretty countryside of that beautiful place, until one terrible day when her father had been killed in a farming accident. After this, her mother had struggled to look after the family alone. Mrs Oberto mentioned having had some help from a 'friend' to cope during this difficult time, but for some reason she wouldn't tell Hannah any details about who the mysterious 'friend' was. She went on to tell Hannah that many years later she had married but had had no children. After her husband had died some years ago, Mrs Oberto had been invited by her sister, who had since moved to England, to travel across Europe and come and live with her. Mrs Oberto had accepted the offer and moved to England, but when her sister died the following year, she had found herself once again living alone.

Mrs Oberto always seemed more cheerful when she was talking about the happy days of her early childhood, before her father had died, so Hannah encouraged her friend to tell her more. As time went by, Mrs Oberto told Hannah many entertaining and colourful stories about these wonderful times from her childhood back in Sicily, but there were two things that Hannah could not get her to talk about. Mrs Oberto would not tell her anything about the mysterious friend who had helped her after her father had died, and she also refused to tell Hannah what was in the old wooden chest that still stood on her bedside table.

Hannah puzzled over this last mystery. She often thought about how tearful Mrs Oberto had been on that first day, when Dad had carried the wooden chest into the bedroom. Surely that must mean that there was something in it that was important. Hannah was intrigued, but she knew that she had to respect Mrs Oberto's privacy, and not ask too many questions.

She got into the habit of going to see Mrs Oberto, as well Mrs Beetle, before leaving for school in the mornings, and she often popped in to see them again after school as well. Sometimes she saw the two ladies at the same time, as Mrs Beetle had taken it upon herself to 'see that Mrs Oberto was alright', as she liked to say. The two old ladies often sat together over a cup of tea in Mrs Oberto's room, and despite their many differences, they became good friends.

One day after school, Hannah finally had some news about her new school history topic.

'It's the ancient Romans, Mrs Oberto!' she said excitedly. 'I've always wanted to learn about them.'

Mrs Oberto seemed strangely excited about it, too, and her head jerked up, her dark eyes gleaming. 'The Romans, Hannah?'

'Yes, Mrs Oberto. Are you also interested in the Romans?' Hannah thought it would be great if Mrs Oberto wanted to help her with her school home-work project.

'The Romans…' Mrs Oberto lifted her head, shook back her black headscarf and gazed into the distance for a moment, as though thinking about some special memory. After a while she smiled gently at Hannah and patted the old wooden chest on her bedside table. 'I know much about them,' she said, her rich accent making the words sound exciting and full of promise. 'Of course the Romans came to your country too, Hannah, but they started nearer to my homeland. They left many ruins in Sicily.'

Of course! Italy was the home of the Romans, and Sicily was right at the foot of the Italian mainland, so Mrs Oberto would be likely to know lots about it all. 'Did you study the Romans at school, Mrs Oberto, just like I'm going to do?' asked Hannah.

'More than that,' replied Mrs Oberto, drawing her black woollen shawl more tightly around her head. 'But you do not need to know where I got my knowledge from, for it to be useful to you.' She touched the silver key hanging on its pink ribbon round her neck. She often did this when she needed reassurance about something.

'So, Hannah – the Romans,' Mrs Oberto said softly, with a secretive smile. 'What do you need to know?'

Chapter 6

Over the next two weeks Hannah started to research the Romans. Her homework project was to choose a person, such as a soldier, a servant or a child, and learn all about what their life might have been like in those long-ago days. Mrs Oberto had suggested that it might be interesting to learn about what life was like for a Roman girl of Hannah's own age. Hannah loved this idea, and started work straight away, sometimes researching her project on the internet, and sometimes listening for hours to Mrs Oberto's slow, deep voice, telling her all manner of interesting facts.

Hannah learnt that the children of Roman working families didn't usually go to school, and that Roman girls would be expected to help their mothers at home. But she also learnt that life for Roman children wasn't all boring, and that they did have toys such as wooden dolls and board games, even if they were poor.

Every evening after school, Mrs Oberto would invite Hannah to her room, and the two of them would sit together, poring over books, sheets of paper, and

Mum's laptop. Dad joked that Mrs Oberto should start charging Hannah for all the help that she was giving her, and said that if Hannah got a good mark at the end of it all, she should tell her teacher that Mrs Oberto deserved a good mark too.

Working on the Roman project seemed to give Mrs Oberto a new lease of life, and she was often sitting ready at her table, her black head scarf pushed back and her dark eyes shining, when Hannah arrived at her room each evening after tea.

Together they made a poster all about childhood in ancient Roman times, drew and coloured pictures of Roman children's clothes, and made a map of where all the Roman temples had been in Mrs Oberto's homeland of Sicily.

One evening Hannah was thinking about Roman hairstyles, and she wondered how the Roman girl she was describing for her project would have worn her hair. 'What do you think, Mrs Oberto?' she asked. 'I've seen pictures of Roman ladies with lovely braided hairstyles. I think I'll draw my Roman girl with a fancy braid in her hair.'

'No, Hannah,' replied Mrs Oberto firmly, frowning slightly. 'Roman girls did not braid their hair, not until they were grown up. Your Roman girl would have worn her hair long and loose.'

'Are you sure?' asked Hannah, a bit disappointed. 'I really want to draw my girl with a nice braid round her head. I'm sure she would have been allowed to have her hair like that if she'd wanted to.'

'Well, you must do as you please,' retorted Mrs

Oberto. 'Tanaquil would never have had her hair up like that at your age.'

Hannah was confused. Who was Tanaquil? Mrs Oberto seemed more short-tempered than usual today, but also she wasn't making any sense. 'That's a strange name. Who's she?'

Mrs Oberto's frown deepened. 'Oh, it is nothing, Hannah, do not worry about it. I was thinking about someone I used to know.'

'But what does she have to do with the Romans?' persisted Hannah, intrigued. She was aware that she was irritating Mrs Oberto by asking more questions, but her curiosity drove her on.

'Oh, I told you it is nothing. Go and leave me now, I am tired!' Mrs Oberto's deep voice was suddenly loud and her face was angry. 'I do not want to help you now.' Abruptly, she pulled her head scarf back up over her head and turned away from Hannah, her shaky hand reaching up to gently touch the key that hung round her neck.

Hannah felt surprised and hurt by Mrs Oberto's reaction, and before she could stop herself she found herself snapping back. 'Suit yourself then, Mrs Oberto, I'll get someone else to help me.' She gathered her papers together in silence and left Mrs Oberto's room, stomping angrily upstairs to the flat, into her bedroom and banging the door. How horrible of Mrs Oberto to speak so unkindly to her. She had only been asking questions, after all. And whoever was this Tanaquil? At least her own questions made sense, which was more than she could say for whatever Mrs Oberto had been talking about.

Chapter 7

Hannah didn't sleep well that night, and the next morning she woke up late. She still felt a bit annoyed with Mrs Oberto, but having had some time to think about it she wasn't as upset as she had been the evening before. The poor lady had been through a lot recently. Hannah wondered guiltily if she should try to be more understanding. Maybe working on the Roman project was too tiring for Mrs Oberto. After all, even though she had been keen to get involved, she was supposed to be in the nursing home for a rest.

That morning Hannah had no time to see either Mrs Oberto or Mrs Beetle. After a hasty breakfast she hurried off to school, deciding that she would say sorry to Mrs Oberto as soon as she got home.

School was busy that day. There was no Roman project work, but lots of tricky maths to get through and, worst of all, a geography test. Hannah knew that she had done badly on the test. She couldn't concentrate properly on the questions in front of her. The idea of thinking about which rivers were the longest didn't seem interesting at all, when the argument with Mrs Oberto was so much on her mind. Added to that, Lucy was off sick, so she couldn't even talk to her about it.

Hannah's eyes were on the classroom clock all day, and she breathed a sigh of relief as the final bell went. Walking quickly home, she decided to stop at the newsagents to get a bar of Mrs Oberto's favourite chocolate. Hopefully it would be accepted as a peace offering and they could be friends again. As she came out of the shop an ambulance whizzed past with its siren blaring. Hannah stuck her fingers in her ears with annoyance. The school was close to a hospital so she was used to the sound, but that didn't stop it hurting her ears.

She continued on her way home. As she rounded the final corner, she was surprised to see the front door of the nursing home standing open. This was strange, as Mum, Dad and the other staff were usually careful to keep it closed, 'to stop the heat getting out', as Mum always said. For some reason Hannah started to feel uneasy, and this feeling increased as she went inside the house, carefully clicking the front door shut behind her.

She walked down the corridor towards the office. Could a quick chat with mum dispel the strange, uneasy feeling that had come upon her? But when she got there the office door was firmly closed.

'You can't go in,' Joanne called, spotting her from the open door of the lounge. 'Your mum's in there talking to the doctor.'

'Why's that?' called back Hannah. 'Doesn't Dr Hayes usually come on Wednesdays?'

'Oh, the new lady's had a stroke,' shouted back Joanne, unfeelingly. 'She went off to hospital in an ambulance a few minutes ago.'

Oh no! Hannah couldn't believe it. She felt numb, and slightly dizzy. Surely nothing could have happened to Mrs Oberto? What if it had been Hannah's fault, for letting her friend get angry and upset last night? Whatever could she do? Hannah didn't know what a stroke was, but it sounded as though Mrs Oberto were seriously ill. What if she died?

Tears sprang into her eyes. Mrs Oberto had become such a good friend, or at least had been a friend until their silly argument the day before. Hannah thought anxiously about what a lovely kind lady Mrs Oberto was, and how much time she had spent helping her with her homework, even if she could be a bit crotchety at times. As memories of the argument flitted back into Hannah's mind, she sat down on the floor outside the office, her hands clasped around her ankles and her back pressed against the wall, hoping desperately that everything would be alright. She gulped back tears as she realised that Mrs Oberto must have been in the ambulance that had sped past her on her way home.

After what seemed like a long time the office door finally opened, and Dr Hayes came out, followed by Mum. Mum looked surprised to see Hannah sitting on the floor in the corridor, and she raised her eyebrows, before ushering the doctor towards the hall. As soon as the front door had closed behind him, Hannah jumped up off the floor. 'Mum... Mrs Oberto... Is Mrs Oberto really ill?' she stammered.

Chapter 8

Mum put her arm round Hannah and guided her gently into the office, closing the door behind them. 'Poor Mrs Oberto started feeling slightly unwell this morning,' she explained quietly. 'I called Dr Hayes and asked if he could pop in to see her afternoon, but then at three o'clock, just as the doctor arrived, she collapsed. I knew it was a stroke straight away, as she couldn't move one side of her body.'

Hannah gulped. 'What's a stroke, Mum?'

Mum stroked her hair. 'It's when a blood clot forms, Hannah, and it stops the blood getting around properly, which can damage the brain. It can sometimes be extremely serious, and it can cause all kinds of problems. Sometimes people can lose the use of their legs, or the ability to speak. We called an ambulance, and she was taken straight off to hospital.' Mum looked at Hannah and sighed as she saw her daughter's eyes fill with tears. 'Oh, Hannah,' she said gently. 'Maybe I shouldn't let you make friends with the residents of the nursing home like this. They're all so old, you know, and these things can happen when people get really old.'

Hannah hardly dared to ask the question. 'She won't die, will she, Mum?' She crossed her fingers while she waited for Mum's reply.

'I don't think so, Hannah.' Mum tapped at her pen nib before continuing. 'The doctor has said that it's likely that she won't be able to walk again, or if she does, it won't be for a long time. She'll need lots of different kinds of medical treatment.'

Hannah let Mum give her a hug, and then she left her to her paperwork and wandered out of the office. It was a lot to take in and she felt as though she needed to talk to someone else about it. She went into the residents' lounge, hoping that Mrs Beetle would be there.

There she was, in her usual chair in the corner, reading another one of her romantic novels. She put it down when she saw Hannah walk in, and patted the chair beside her. For a moment the two sat in silence, before Mrs Beetle quietly asked, 'Did you hear about Mrs Oberto, Grub?'

Usually Mrs Beetle was excited about having something new to gossip about in the nursing home, but not this time. The two old ladies had become close friends over the previous few weeks.

'Yes,' answered Hannah, her eyes filling with tears again.

Mrs Beetle patted her hand. 'Don't worry, Grub,' she said, forcing a smile. 'She might get better, but it's in the lap of the gods now, you know.'

'What do you mean?' Hannah asked.

'Oh, it's just something you say. It means we can't do anything about it. We just have to wait and see what happens.'

They sat together companionably and quietly for a while, both thinking about Mrs Oberto, before Mrs Beetle broke the silence. 'Are you planning to visit her, Grub?'

'I'd like to, if I'm allowed.'

'Well, if you do, give her my best wishes, won't you?' A tear rolled down Mrs Beetle's wrinkled cheek. 'I'll miss our morning chats, until she gets better and comes back.'

'Of course I will,' Hannah said, determined now that she would visit Mrs Oberto in hospital, even if it wasn't really allowed.

Hannah gave Mrs Beetle a promise to keep her updated about Mrs Oberto, and then went upstairs to the flat. As she walked in, she saw Dad sitting at the table, reading the paper. He gave her a smile but as soon as he did so, Hannah burst into fresh tears, sobs shaking her body.

'Oh Dad,' she wailed, 'I think it's my fault for having an argument with her about my school project yesterday.'

Dad didn't need to ask what Hannah was talking about. 'Now, come on,' he said, pulling her into a hug. 'Strokes don't happen because of arguments, you know. These things happen because of health reasons. It's nothing to do with you. I know that you must feel worried about her though. You've become so close to her since she arrived.' He smoothed Hannah's hair away from her wet face. 'Shall I find out if she can have visitors?'

Hannah stopped crying, rubbed her face with the tissue Dad offered, and sniffed loudly. 'Yes please,' she whispered.

As Dad went off to phone the hospital, Hannah sat down in his empty chair. She put her hand in her pocket, and felt something there. It was the bar of chocolate that she had bought for Mrs Oberto. It was starting to melt and was just beginning to ooze out through the silver wrapping. Hannah threw it into the bin along with her damp tissue, and then gave a hard, determined sniff. Mrs Oberto had to get better. She just had to.

Chapter 9

When Dad finished on the phone he had some good news. The hospital had said that they were happy for Mrs Oberto to have a visitor that evening, as long as it was not for too long. What a relief! Did this mean that Mrs Oberto's stroke hadn't been as bad as the doctors had first thought? Hannah felt delighted that she could go to visit and apologise for the argument they had had the evening before, even though that somehow felt like weeks ago now.

Hannah thought about the melted chocolate that she'd just thrown away. She'd have to get something else to take as a present for Mrs Oberto now. Feeling a bit brighter, she went up to her room to change out of her school uniform, and while she was changing she glanced around. Did she have anything that would make a good gift? Eventually her eye was caught by something that she had brought home from school the day before.

Earlier that week, Hannah and her class had made Roman-style pendants out of cardboard, spraying them with metallic paint to make them look as if they were made of bronze, as the real Roman ones would have been. When the paint was dry, they'd hung them from leather cords so they could be worn as necklaces. Hannah's pendant was shaped like an upside-down crescent moon. She'd copied it from a picture she'd seen in a library book about the Romans, where she had read that this particular style of Roman pendant was called a 'lunula'. Apparently it was the type of thing that a young Roman girl might have worn for good luck. Hannah had decided to put it in with her school homework project, but homework didn't seem quite so important anymore. She'd give it to Mrs Oberto.

She carefully wrapped the delicate cardboard pendant and its cord in a hankie, and put the little package in her pocket. Hannah put her shoulders back in a determined manner. She would ask Mum if she could go to the hospital straight away.

When she got to the office, Mum was looking stressed. 'If Dad's checked it's okay, then yes, you can, Hannah, but please don't stay too long,' said Mum, flicking her pen nib absentmindedly in the way she always did when she was worried about something. 'If you're going, please can you remember to ask the hospital if they'd like us to send anything else in for her, while you're there? It'll save me a phone call.'

Hannah promised Mum she would, and set off straight away, feeling the curve of the cardboard pendant through the hankie in her pocket as she went. The hospital was only a short walk from the nursing home, but it wasn't until she arrived that Hannah realised she didn't know which ward Mrs Oberto was on. Feeling annoyed with herself for not having asked Dad before she left home, she went up the hospital steps, in through the main front door, and up to the smartly dressed lady behind the reception desk.

'Mrs Oberto?' The lady pressed a few keys on her keyboard. 'Oh yes, here we are – she came in today. Christina Oberto – she's on Ward Four.'

Hannah looked at the sign that swung creakily from the ceiling, and then followed the directions to Ward Four, her footsteps echoing as she went up some draughty stairs and then down a long, white corridor. Eventually she found herself outside some double swing doors with a big sign hanging above them. 'Welcome to Ward Four'. Hannah felt a bit nervous. She hoped Mrs Oberto would be pleased to see her. What if she was still angry, after their argument?

Pushing the heavy doors open, Hannah walked hesitantly into the ward. As soon as she came through the doors, she was dazzled by a sunbeam coming in through a large window. Blinking, she squinted into the sun, just able to make out a desk in front of her. She walked up to it and, shading her eyes with her hand, took a deep breath before clearing her throat. 'Excuse me, I've come to visit Mrs Oberto,' she said nervously.

Chapter 10

The nurse behind the desk wore a dark blue uniform with a watch pinned to the top pocket, and she was reading some typed notes. All in all she had a very serious and important air. Hannah felt more nervous than ever, and she thrust her hand back into her pocket and clutched the cardboard pendant in the hankie tightly for reassurance. After a moment the nurse put down the notes and looked up, showing an unexpectedly friendly, smiling face. Hannah felt relieved and she relaxed a little as she explained why she had come.

'Mrs Oberto?' queried the nurse. 'Are you a relative?'

'I'm not,' replied Hannah, suddenly thinking that this might have been the wrong thing to say, if she wanted to be allowed into the ward. 'But I am from the nursing home where she's living,' she continued quickly. 'My dad did ring to check if I could visit her for a few minutes, and someone told him it would be okay.' She looked pleadingly at the nurse.

'Don't worry,' said the nurse reassuringly. 'I'm sure it'd be lovely for her to see you for a few minutes. She's had a frightening experience today. Now that we've got her settled in bed I'm sure seeing a familiar friendly face would do her good.'

She took Hannah's arm, turned her round and pointed down the ward. 'Can you see that bed at the end? The one below the window?'

'Yes, thank you.' Hannah set off nervously down the long ward.

Now that she'd got past the nurse, she was feeling anxious again about what kind of reception she would get from Mrs Oberto. But as she got closer to the end bed, she felt less concerned about herself and more worried about her friend. Now she was nearly there she could see that Mrs Oberto was wired up to all kinds of medical equipment, and even had an oxygen mask over her face. She was wearing a hospital nightdress, but Hannah noticed that she still wore the silver key on its pink ribbon around her neck. She seemed to be lying back on a mound of pillows with her eyes closed. Could she be asleep?

She felt shy about going too close to the bed with all the equipment around it. Somehow it made Mrs Oberto seem like a stranger, distanced from Hannah by buzzing electrical boxes and trailing wires.

Hannah paused at the end of the bed. Should she wake Mrs Oberto up? Even if she tried to get close enough to wake her, she'd be frightened of knocking over some important equipment. Perhaps she should go back to the desk and ask someone what to do. She was just turning away to see if she could still see the nurse, when she heard a familiar voice.

'Is that you, Hannah?' Mrs Oberto had pulled off the oxygen mask to speak. Now that it was removed, she looked more like her normal self.

'Oh, Mrs Oberto, are you alright?' Hannah gasped, noticing that Mrs Oberto's Italian accent was slurred in a way it hadn't been before, as though she were speaking underwater.

'I will be.' Mrs Oberto was speaking slowly to make her voice as clear as possible. 'This stroke has made it hard to talk, but the doctor says I have been lucky not to lose my speech completely.' She tried to move into a more comfortable position in the bed, and flinched as she did so. 'I am frightened, Hannah. I cannot move my legs, and the doctors say they might not get better.'

Hannah shifted uneasily from foot to foot. How awful for Mrs Oberto if she could never walk again. She took a deep breath. 'I really want you to get better, Mrs Oberto, and so does Mrs Beetle – she asked me to tell you,' she said, speaking quickly. 'I want to ask you more about how you are, but first I need to say that I'm so sorry we had an argument yesterday evening.' She paused to see how Mrs Oberto would react, and felt shocked when the old lady gave a deep chuckle.

'I am sorry too, Hannah, but you should know by now my fiery temper and quick words. They mean nothing. Can we agree to say no more about it, and be friends again? I am so sorry also.'

Hannah felt so relieved she didn't know what to say next, but then she remembered the cardboard pendant in her pocket. 'I've brought you something I made in school,' she said, as she pulled out the hankie and unwrapped the pendant.

Mrs Oberto's eyes opened wide with surprise. 'You brought this for me?' she asked gruffly, seeming to try to speak clearly and hide her emotions at the same time.

'Yes. I hope it will make you feel better, Mrs Oberto. I thought you might like a present.'

'It is lovely, Hannah, thank you!' Mrs Oberto looked thoughtful for a moment, and then continued to speak slowly and carefully in her deep Italian accent, as though considering each word's worth before setting it free. 'Now I know that you are the right person for me to trust with my secret, Hannah.' She glanced around to check they were alone, before fixing her dark eyes on Hannah's face. 'I need you to see something that I have never shown to anyone else.'

Chapter 11

Hannah could feel the seriousness of the moment. Drawn forwards by Mrs Oberto's powerful gaze, she stepped closer to the bed, the medical equipment around them forgotten.

'Hannah, I want you to open the wooden chest in my bedroom,' Mrs Oberto went on slowly. 'You must take out what it contains. Hold it in your hands and allow it to speak to you, as it did to me when I was your age.'

Hannah was intrigued, but also worried. Had the stroke affected Mrs Oberto's mind as well as her body and voice? 'What do you mean?' she whispered, glancing around her. A group of doctors was starting to make their way down the ward, stopping at each bed in turn.

'Hannah, in the chest is something precious. Something that can help in times of trouble. It helped me as a frightened young girl to cope with my father's death, and if you hold it in your two hands, it might speak to you, too, and tell you how to help me to get better. You are so similar in many ways to me as a young girl…' Mrs Oberto's voice trailed off. The strain of trying to speak clearly was beginning to show.

The doctors were at the next bed now. 'Don't worry, Mrs Oberto, you can trust me,' Hannah whispered seriously. As their eyes met once more, it felt as if something important and secret had passed between them.

Mrs Oberto smiled. Then she reached up, pulled the pink ribbon over her head and held out the dangling key to Hannah. 'You had better get home now before I shout at you again,' she said, speaking slowly and hoarsely but winking at Hannah reassuringly. As the doctors arrived and surrounded Mrs Oberto's bed, Hannah took the key, slipped the pink ribbon around her own neck, pushed it under her jumper out of sight, and slipped away. She walked quickly. Back down the ward, along the corridor, down the draughty stairs and out through the main reception, into the fresh air.

Walking home, Hannah thought about what Mrs Oberto had said. What was the strange thing in the wooden chest that Mrs Oberto thought might speak to her, and how could it possibly help anyone, either in the past when Mrs Oberto was a girl, or now, when she was old and ill?

As soon as she got home, Hannah realised that she had forgotten to do the one thing her mum had asked her to do. Find out from the ward nurse if Mrs Oberto needed anything else brought in to the hospital. Oh well, she'd just have to own up and admit she had forgotten, although she couldn't tell her parents why.

She wanted to go straight to Mrs Oberto's room to look inside the wooden chest, but as she walked past the office door, Mum stuck out her head. As soon as Mum heard that Hannah had forgotten to ask the nurse if there was anything else that Mrs Oberto needed, she told her crossly to go straight upstairs for tea.

As she sat eating fish fingers with Dad, Hannah answered his questions about the hospital absent-mindedly. She was thinking all the time of how quickly she could get back downstairs.

Dad gave a comforting smile. 'Would you like a chocolate muffin for pudding, Hannah? I thought it might cheer you up as you were a bit upset earlier?'

'No thanks, Dad, I'm okay.' Hannah put her hand up and felt the shape of the silver key through her jumper. 'I'm feeling much better now, but I'll have a muffin later, if that's okay?'

'Don't worry. I often go off my food, too, when I'm feeling worried.' Dad smiled understandingly. Hannah smiled back, knowing that she couldn't tell him the real reason she was so keen for tea to finish. She usually offered to help Dad do the dishes in the evenings, and she dutifully but reluctantly picked up the tea towel as Dad pushed back his chair and carried the plates to the sink.

'Don't worry about it tonight, Hannah,' Dad said gently, patting her on the shoulder. 'You go off and relax for a bit.'

Hannah was so pleased that she nearly forgot to say thanks. Then, trying not to look too excited, she walked quickly back downstairs into the nursing home and towards the door of Mrs Oberto's room. What was she about to find?

Chapter 12

As she put her hand on the door handle, Hannah remembered how excited she'd been when she'd come to say hello to Mrs Oberto for the first time. How scary that deep voice had sounded, heard through the door, and how dark the room had been when she'd first walked in.

The bedroom looked very different now. The assistant nurses had been in to tidy up, which was something that Mrs Oberto never usually allowed. The curtains had been neatly drawn against the falling darkness outside, the bed made, the pillows plumped and all the bits and pieces put away. In some ways the room looked much nicer, but in other ways it seemed to have been stripped of Mrs Oberto's personality. It almost looked like a different room. Almost, but not quite, because there on the bedside table was the thing that she had come to find – the old wooden chest.

Hannah walked over and put her hand on the lid of the chest. What had Mrs Oberto said was inside? Something precious, that could help in times of trouble.

Something that could maybe even speak to her. She couldn't possibly imagine what it might be, but she allowed her curiosity to get the better of her nerves. Taking the pink ribbon from around her neck, she held her breath and fitted the key into the fancy silver lock.

The key turned easily. As the lid fell back, Hannah gasped. In contrast to the old, battered, dark wood that the outside of the chest was made of, the inside looked as though it had always been protected and cared for. Almost against her will, Hannah felt drawn to look in, and leaning forwards she saw a lining of pale, golden, highly polished wood that seemed to emit a soft light all of its own, shining onto her face, warming her cheeks and dazzling her eyes. At first the chest seemed empty, but as her eyes adjusted to the strange, eerie glow, Hannah noticed just one object lying at the bottom. An old envelope. It was slightly ripped at the corners, and quite dirty, as though it had been stepped on a few times by someone wearing muddy shoes.

Plucking up her courage, Hannah picked up the envelope. She could feel something small, hard and flat inside it. Maybe metal of some kind, or possibly jewellery? The envelope wasn't sealed and she turned it upside down, tipping the object out into her hand.

She blinked with surprise. Lying on the palm of her hand was a crescent-moon-shaped pendant. A 'lunula' pendant, as she knew the Romans had called them. It was almost identical to the cardboard one she had given to Mrs Oberto, just a short time ago, but this one was much thinner and finer. It was small and made of a dull gold-coloured metal. Could it be real bronze? Although it was smooth on the back, it looked extremely old. Holding it up, Hannah could make out some scratches on it. Peering even closer, she could also see some clearer lines etched in the form of a pattern onto the front of the pendant.

Could this be a genuine Roman bronze object? It certainly looked similar to the Roman one she had seen photographed in the library book at school. Hannah carried the pendant over to the table lamp to look at it more closely. As the light fell onto the pendant's surface, she wondered if some of the fainter scratch marks could have been caused by being buried in the soil, maybe for over two thousand years, until it had been rediscovered. She might be holding the oldest thing that she had ever touched!

In her fascination with the pendant, Hannah had almost forgotten what else Mrs Oberto had said to her, but now she remembered. Mrs Oberto had said that she should 'hold it in her two hands'. Hannah had had the pendant resting in the palm of one hand, but now she decided that a serious moment had come. A moment for her to find out if Mrs Oberto was confused as a result of her stroke, or whether there really was something special about this pendant. Could it really speak to her and offer help? Smiling to herself, feeling a bit silly and glad that no one else was watching, Hannah closed her two hands around the pendant and then stood completely still, waiting to see if anything would happen.

Chapter 13

At first nothing happened, and after a minute or so Hannah began to feel disappointed. She was just starting to think that maybe she should go back upstairs to the flat, when she noticed that her hands felt slightly warmer than they had done before. Was she just imagining this, though? Was it nothing but wishful thinking? But after another few seconds she knew something was definitely happening. The pendant was now really hot and getting more so all the time. Soon it was uncomfortable to hold – she would have to put it down before her hands were burnt. Quickly, she dropped it onto the bedside table. The pendant was really glowing now, and the etched pattern of lines seemed to be fading away as it blazed hotter and brighter, glowing first a dazzling yellow and then a vibrant, fiery red.

She stared, wide-eyed with amazement. Whatever was happening was certainly something very far from ordinary. She bent over the pendant, watching it glow until it became so bright that she could no longer look directly at it. She put her hand over her eyes. What if it got so hot that the bedside table caught fire? Hannah squinted through her fingers to see what was happening, and as she did so, noticed that the glow was changing. She bent closer and closer to the little pendant. The heat seemed to be fading, but not the brightness. The surface was becoming so smooth, it was almost like a tiny mirror. It was so shiny that Hannah thought she could see the reflection of her own face, framed by her long loose brown hair, looking back at her. Or was it her own face? She looked more closely and then noticed something. The face in the pendant was smiling – but Hannah wasn't. It couldn't be her reflection, after all, but the face of someone else.

Hannah didn't understand the magic that had happened, but she was sure of one thing. Someone else was looking out at her from inside the pendant.

Amazed, Hannah looked at the smiling face peering out at her from the pendant's smooth surface. The girl she saw looked similar to her in many ways, but the longer she looked, the more she realised that it wasn't only the smile that was different. Although the long, brown hair was the same, the eyes in the pendant were slightly darker, and so was the skin. Hannah glanced briefly over at Mrs Oberto's pillowcase, keen to reassure herself that the rest of the room was still normal. It was. She looked back again and the smiling face was still there.

So this was the friend that Mrs Oberto had spoken of, the one who had helped her to cope after her father had died. This must be the person that Mrs Oberto hoped might be able to help her to get better.

Ignoring the butterflies in her stomach, Hannah smiled shyly. The girl in the pendant smiled back more

44

broadly. Hannah, encouraged by this, pulled all her courage together, took a deep breath and said, 'Hello.'

It wasn't much but at least it was a start. Would the girl reply, and if so, would Hannah be able to understand or even hear her?

'Greetings,' replied the girl in a clear voice. Hannah gulped. She was surprised that such a normal voice could come from the tiny pendant.

'Hello,' repeated Hannah. Whatever should she say next? Thoughts whizzing wildly around in her head, she plumped for the first question that came into her mind. 'Who are you, and how are you able to speak to me?'

'My name is Tanaquil. I am named after an ancient Roman queen. It is a long time since I have been called upon to speak, but I am glad to meet you. What is your name?'

'I'm Hannah.' Funnily enough, the conversation was already beginning to feel more normal. 'The pendant belongs to my friend, Mrs Oberto. Have you spoken to her in the past?'

'I have not,' answered Tanaquil, looking surprised. 'I had believed that the pendant still belonged to my friend Christina, a girl I once helped when she was in trouble and distress.'

Suddenly Hannah remembered what the lady at the hospital reception desk had said, when she'd looked up Mrs Oberto on her computer. 'Christina Oberto'.

'Christina! Yes, that is Mrs Oberto,' Hannah said excitedly. 'But she's an old lady now. Did the pendant originally belong to you?' Eagerly, she watched Tanaquil's face in the pendant, waiting for an answer.

Chapter 14

'Yes, the pendant was mine,' Tanaquil replied. 'I lived in Sicily, a country ruled over by the Romans. It was usual there for girls to wear such pendants for good luck, and I was given mine by my parents when I was a small child.'

'What happened after that?' asked Hannah breathlessly.

Tanaquil looked sad. 'One day my mother asked me to take some food to my father who was working in the fields. When I got home my pendant was gone. The cord that held it round my neck had broken. My mother was angry and sent me back to look for it, but it had vanished.' She frowned at the distressing memory. 'My mother and I prayed to the gods for it to be found, but it never was. I worried that without it I would have no good luck in life.'

'Did you?' Hannah asked, entranced.

'My mother took me to the temple, and we prayed before the statues of the gods, hoping that with their help, the loss of the pendant would not affect my luck in life,' answered Tanaquil. 'And so it was for some years. My life was fortunate until I reached the age of twelve years old. Then, to my parents' horror, I became ill with a fever and died.'

'I'm so sorry for you.' Hannah's brain reeled at the thought that this girl had died, but her heart was also heavy with sympathy for her new friend. 'I suppose there wasn't much good medicine in those days, was there?'

'Medicine and doctors are no good to anyone,' answered Tanaquil with feeling. 'To truly recover from illness you can only pray before the statues of the gods in the temple. For illness it is the god of medicine and healing to whom you should pray. Sadly my parents were not able to take me to the temple to be healed by him in time to save me.'

It seemed that Tanaquil was becoming quite angry at the idea of doctors and medicine, so Hannah decided to try to change the subject, and she asked a question that was really puzzling her. 'Tanaquil, however did you manage to first speak through the pendant to Mrs Oberto – I mean, Christina?'

Tanaquil's eyes took on a dreamy, faraway expression. 'One day, many years – possibly even more than a thousand years – after I had died, I felt myself awakening and being pulled, as though away from death. I found myself looking through what seemed to be a mirror. Then I realised it was the pendant I had valued so much.' She paused to brush her hair away from her face, and Hannah saw that her eyes were bright with tears as she remembered what had happened.

'Hovering in front of me I could see the image of a girl who looked similar to me, and she was crying, as I am now at the memory of these things.' Tanaquil forced a weak smile. 'She told me that her name was Christina. Her father had died, and she felt so sad but had no friends to speak to about it. She had found the pendant while digging in her mother's garden. It seemed that holding it tightly in her hands while she was in need of support had called me back to the edge of your world, to help her.'

Hannah listened with fascination as Tanaquil told her how she had agreed to be there for Christina to talk to, and how the two girls had become friends and shared many stories with each other. Months later, when Christina began to recover from the sadness of losing her father, her need for help had begun to fade, and at the same time the pendant's ability to link her to her Roman friend had also become weaker. Finally, for Christina at least, Tanaquil had gone.

Chapter 15

Hannah knew that the time had come to tell Tanaquil about Mrs Oberto's health problems. 'Christina needs you again now, Tanaquil,' she said. 'She's asked me to call you back, through the pendant. She's ill and needs help to recover. Is there anything you can do?'

'What has happened?' asked Tanaquil quickly, her eyes widening.

'She's in hospital. The doctors are trying to help her to recover, but she's had something called a stroke, and we don't know if she will be able to walk again,' explained Hannah, wondering as she spoke, what help Tanaquil could possibly provide. It was one thing to support a friend who needed someone to talk to, as Tanaquil had when Mrs Oberto had been a girl, but this situation was different. Surely Tanaquil wouldn't be able to help her now?

'Doctors?' said Tanaquil bitterly. 'They could not help me to get better, and rarely helped anyone to recover from illness in my world. No, the only thing to do is to take Christina to the temple, and have her sleep under a statue of the god of healing and medicine.' As she spoke, her face began to fade, as though having given Hannah the information she needed, her help was no longer required.

'No, wait!' called Hannah. 'What is the god's name?' But it was too late. Tanaquil's face slowly faded away, until finally the pendant had returned to its usual bronze colour and looked just as it had when Hannah had first shaken it out of its envelope.

Hannah felt very unsure. Surely Tanaquil hadn't given her the right answer at all. What could she possibly do? There were certainly no Roman temples in the town where she lived, and not even any museums where a Roman statue might be found, as far as she knew.

The excitement and amazement Hannah had felt during the magical experience of speaking to a real Roman girl from the past was quickly fading, as she realised that she might be no closer to finding any help for Mrs Oberto. Of course, she couldn't really blame Tanaquil. How could a Roman girl be expected to know that so much had changed since she had been alive two thousand years ago?

Hannah put the pendant back into its dirty envelope, laid it gently on the glowing lining inside the chest, closed the lid and locked it. She put the key round her neck again to keep it safe, and went back upstairs to her bedroom in the flat. After getting ready for bed, she lay down to think about the incredible experience that had just happened. She could hardly believe the events of the last hour. Would she ever be able to find out which god Tanaquil had been talking about? She found a scrap of paper and a pencil in her bedside table and wrote down 'Roman god of healing and medicine'. Lying down again, she began to wonder what this strange god had looked like. Maybe it would help if she knew what she was looking for. She fell asleep, resolving that the next day she would look up the god on the internet and, if possible, find a picture of him.

The next morning was a Saturday, so there was no school. Once Hannah was up she had a quick breakfast with Dad in the flat, and then made her way downstairs to the office. She wondered if she would be able to persuade Mum to let her use her laptop. Sometimes Mum let her, but it all depended on how busy she was. Hannah crossed her fingers. If she was lucky Mum would have some free time and would be in a helpful mood.

Chapter 16

'Can I use the laptop, Mum?' asked Hannah. 'I need to look up some Roman things for school.'

Mum smiled. 'Of course you can. Sit with me and use it in here if you like. With Mrs Oberto in hospital for a while, you might need some extra help with your homework. I know she's been an enthusiastic helper with your Roman project.'

'Yes, she has. Mum, you've nursed lots of people after strokes. Do you think Mrs Oberto will get back the use of her legs?'

Mum put her arm round Hannah and sat in silence for a few moments. At last she said, 'Well, people do get better sometimes after strokes, especially if they get lots of help from all the medical people at the hospital, but it can take a long time. There's always a high risk of not getting better at all.' She gave Hannah a squeeze. 'Mrs Oberto has had a serious stroke you know, Hannah. We need to remember that she might not get better as much or as quickly as you'd like.'

Hannah gulped silently, and thought of Mrs Oberto lying in her hospital bed, surrounded by wires and machines. She didn't get this attached to all the people who lived in the nursing home, but there were some people, like Mrs Beetle and Mrs Oberto, whom she just couldn't help becoming friends with. She cared about them as though they were members of her family.

Mum set up the laptop and asked what Hannah needed to find out for her homework. Hannah explained that she wanted to find a picture of the Roman god of healing and medicine. After a few false starts they came across an article called 'Aesculapius – the Roman god of healing and medicine'. Hannah rolled the strange name around on her tongue. 'Ess-cul-a-pea-us' seemed to be the most likely way to pronounce it. Scrolling down through the article, she found a picture of a statue of the god. He looked like a serious old man, in a Roman toga. He was holding a long stick with a snake twisted around it.

'Good thing he can't jump off the screen at us. Look at that horrid-looking pet snake he's got there,' laughed Mum, who hated snakes. 'You'd better be careful, you know. If you print it off and leave it in your room, you could get a nasty snake bite.' She chuckled again at her own joke, and then turned back to her paperwork, leaving Hannah to carry on by herself for a while.

As Hannah switched on the printer, the words that Mum had just said floated around in her mind. Of course, Mum had been joking about the snake coming alive on the page if it was printed off, but what if a picture of the god of healing and medicine would be enough to help Mrs Oberto? Tanaquil had said that Roman people would go to the temple and sleep under a statue of this god, but what if Mrs Oberto slept under a picture of his statue? Could that have the same effect?

Hannah reached over to the printer, picked up the sheet of paper with the picture on it and dashed upstairs to her room. She searched through her dressing-table drawers until she found a blank card and a glue stick, and then she quickly cut out the picture of the statue and glued it onto the front of the card. She wrote inside, 'To Mrs Oberto, get well soon, with love from Hannah and Tanaquil'. Slipping it into an envelope, she pulled on her coat. She dashed downstairs to ask Mum if she could pop up to the hospital to visit Mrs Oberto before lunch.

'If you've finished your homework, that's fine,' agreed Mum, smiling. 'Maybe you can take her these flowers as well. They're from all of us at the home, to make her feel better. It was Mrs Beetle's idea.'

Hannah took the big bunch of pink and white flowers, smiling at Mrs Beetle's thoughtfulness.

She pushed the card she had made into her coat pocket and set off towards the hospital. 'Well,' she said to herself as she walked briskly along. 'Let's see what this Roman god can do.'

Chapter 17

When Hannah arrived at the hospital she made her way straight to the ward. She walked briskly up to the nurse's desk as before, but she was surprised to see that a different nurse was on duty.

The nurse peered unsmilingly at Hannah over the top of her glasses. 'Can I help you?' she asked frostily.

Hannah's hopes of seeing Mrs Oberto and giving her the card began to fade.

'Yes, I've come to see Mrs Oberto. I'm from the nursing home where she lives, and I need to give her these flowers and an important card.' She smiled at the nurse, trying to look more confident than she felt.

'Well, I'm sorry, it's not visiting time just now,' said the nurse, frowning at Hannah and the flowers. 'The doctors are all busy with the patients at the moment, you know.'

Hannah felt crushed with disappointment, but just at that moment a lady in a white doctor's coat walked up to the desk. She smiled at Hannah as she stopped to pick up some medical notes, and on the spur of the moment, Hannah decided to take advantage of this sign of friendliness.

'Excuse me,' she said boldly. 'Are you the doctor looking after Mrs Oberto?'

The doctor's smile broadened. 'Yes, I am. Are you a member of her family?'

'I'm not, but she doesn't have a family and I'm from the nursing home where she lives,' blurted out Hannah, tripping over her words in an effort to keep the attention of the nice doctor. 'I know it's not visiting time, but I just wanted to give her these things, and see how she is.'

The doctor looked kindly at Hannah's pleading face, and then took her arm. She guided her up the ward, away from the furious nurse, towards Mrs Oberto's bed.

'Well,' she said quietly. 'It's not really visiting time now, you know, but it seems that you are as good as family. Would you like to see her for just five minutes?'

'Oh, yes please,' Hannah answered with relief. 'I really just need to give her something, that's all, but first can you tell me how she is?' Her grip tightened on the bunch of flowers as she waited for the doctor's reply.

'She's had a serious stroke, you know,' the doctor said thoughtfully, echoing what Hannah's mum had said earlier. 'It's always possible that as time goes by she might get the use of her legs back, but it would take a long time, and it's quite likely that it might not happen at all.' She looked at Hannah's anxious face. 'I know it's not good news,' she said gently, 'but I don't want to give you any false hope.'

Hannah nodded and smiled as best she could, and the doctor patted her shoulder. 'Just five minutes now, or I'll be in trouble. If she's sleeping, don't wake her.' She marched briskly away, leaving Hannah to walk to the end of the ward by herself.

When Hannah arrived at Mrs Oberto's bedside, she found her asleep. Finding an empty vase on a nearby window sill, she arranged the flowers in it, adding some water from a sink near the bed. She put both the vase of flowers and the card on Mrs Oberto's tray-table. Searching in her still chocolaty pocket, she found a torn piece of paper and a stump of old pencil. Smoothing the paper out, she wrote a short note for Mrs Oberto to read when she woke up.

'The flowers are from Mrs Beetle and everyone else at the home', she wrote. 'Make sure you open the card and put it on your bedside table tonight, so you can sleep under it'.

She pushed the note on top of the card, and checked it was positioned so that Mrs Oberto would see it as soon as she woke up. Then, crossing her fingers, she walked quickly back up the ward. She didn't want to stay too long in case the nice doctor got into trouble with the grumpy nurse. She would just have to wait now, and see if the Roman god was able to do what Tanaquil had promised. As she walked along, she suddenly thought about Mrs Beetle's comment that Mrs Oberto's recovery was 'in the lap of the gods'. Hannah smiled grimly to herself as she thought that Mrs Beetle didn't realise how true this really was.

Chapter 18

When Hannah arrived home she was keen to tell Tanaquil what she had done, and she went straight to Mrs Oberto's room and took out the pendant. However, even though she held it tightly between her hands for nearly ten minutes, the only result was that her hands began to feel all sweaty. She put the pendant back and locked the wooden chest again, feeling disappointed. Her new Roman friend was the only person she felt she could talk to about leaving the card at the hospital, but for now she would have to keep the secret all to herself.

The rest of the day passed slowly and Hannah felt restless. She tried to do some work on her Roman homework project, but it just didn't seem the same without Mrs Oberto to help her, and she soon put it away again. She read a book until that also became boring, and then finally went outside to help Dad sweep up some leaves in the garden. She thought about going back to the hospital at evening visiting time, but decided not to. She was too nervous and preferred to wait until the next day. Then at least she would be able to find out for sure whether the picture of the Roman god had had any effect on Mrs Oberto.

The more Hannah thought about it, the more ridiculous it seemed. How could a picture of a Roman god do more than properly trained doctors and nurses to make someone better? Then she had to remind herself that, only a short time ago, it would have seemed ridiculous that she could have had a conversation with a real Roman girl who had lived two thousand years ago.

Before bedtime, Hannah sat with her parents in the small living room of the upstairs flat. Her mum was having a rare evening off, although she had left the assistant nurses downstairs with strict instructions to call her if there were any problems. Much to her parents' surprise, Hannah decided to have an early night. She had had enough of worrying about what might happen at the hospital, and she wanted to go to sleep and forget all about it for a while.

She fell asleep surprisingly quickly and she slept heavily, dreaming about losing something precious in a field, and walking around for hours, crying. When she woke up on Sunday morning she felt groggy and confused, but then the events of the previous day began to fall back into place in her brain, like pieces in a jigsaw. She looked at the clock and noticed that it was nearly nine o'clock. As she got quickly out of bed, she heard the phone ringing downstairs in the office. As always she heard Mum rushing to answer it, before the shutting of the office door cut off the sound of her voice.

A few minutes later, Hannah was dressed and having some cereal with Dad in the kitchen when Mum walked in, looking pleased but also puzzled.

'I don't understand it,' Mum said, flicking at her pen nib in her usual worried way. 'The hospital just rang and said they're sending Mrs Oberto home today.'

How amazing! Without thinking, Hannah jumped off her chair in delight. 'It's worked!' she shouted, grinning in triumph and waving her cereal spoon in the air.

Both her parents looked at her in confusion, and Mum gave Hannah a strange look.

'Anyway,' Mum continued, frowning slightly, 'they said Mrs Oberto's coming home today. I hope there's not been some mistake. She should have weeks of physiotherapy and medical tests, before they could even think of sending her home. The nurse on the phone didn't give me a chance to ask any questions before she rang off.'

'I'll pop up there, shall I, and see what it's all about?' asked Dad, finishing his coffee and picking up his car keys.

'I'll come with you, Dad,' offered Hannah quickly. 'You might need help carrying things.'

Could it be really true that Mrs Oberto was better? Hannah couldn't wait to get to the hospital to find out.

Chapter 19

In the car on the way to the hospital, Hannah could hardly sit still. She'd have preferred to walk there, so they didn't have to waste time looking for a parking space when they arrived. After all, it was only a few minutes from home. However, Dad had explained that if Mrs Oberto really was coming home that day, she wouldn't be able to walk and would need a wheelchair just to get from the ward to the car. He reminded Hannah that just because Mrs Oberto might be coming home, if didn't mean that she was better. She had just had a stroke, after all.

As Hannah walked with Dad onto the now familiar ward, she saw the friendly nurse that she had met on her first visit. The nurse gave a huge smile when she them. 'Well,' she said excitedly, patting Hannah on the arm, 'weren't we all in for a surprise this morning?'

Hannah smiled at her encouragingly, and the nurse went on. 'Yes, I came in for my shift at seven o'clock this morning, and Mrs Oberto wasn't in her bed.'

'What?' exclaimed Dad. 'Surely they hadn't taken her for some more tests that early in the morning?'

'No,' the nurse replied, jingling her keys in an agitated way as she spoke. 'You won't believe this, but she'd disconnected herself from all the monitors, hopped out of bed and walked off. Of course I was panicking, but one of the other patients told me they'd seen her strolling down to the other end of the ward. I ran down there, expecting to find her on the floor and there she was, coming round the corner towards me. She told me I was making a silly fuss, and that a person should be able to go to the toilet on their own in peace, when they wanted to.'

'But hang on a minute,' spluttered Dad. 'They told us that she'd had a stroke and wouldn't walk again for months, if at all. Did the doctors get it wrong? Wasn't it a stroke after all?'

'Well,' answered the excited nurse, 'the scans all indicated that it was a major stroke, but we're not going to turn down a miracle when it comes along. We'd like her to come back in a few days for some more tests, to be on the safe side, but she's certainly determined to go home today, and we really can't stop her.'

Hannah looked towards the far end of the ward to see her friend sitting fully dressed in a chair at the side of her bed, with her bag packed. When Mrs Oberto saw Hannah she smiled and waved, got up, picked up her bag and, swinging it lightly from her hand, walked confidently and proudly up the ward towards them.

Dad's mouth dropped open, but he soon recovered enough to run down the ward to take Mrs Oberto's bag from her. 'I'll carry that,' he offered, immediately staggering under its unexpected weight. 'Whatever have you got in here, Mrs Oberto?'

'Oh, just a few bits and pieces,' replied Mrs Oberto, her slurred voice now gone, and her Italian accent as deep and rich as it had been on the day when she and Hannah had first met. She smiled and winked at Hannah, and, delighted, Hannah winked back.

When they got out to the car park, Mrs Oberto insisted on sitting on the back seat next to Hannah, but despite Hannah's questions, she wouldn't talk about what had happened on the ward. 'I will tell you all about it when we are back in my room, by ourselves,' she hissed.

As soon as they got back to the nursing home, Hannah wanted to go with Mrs Oberto to her room straight away, to hear what had happened. Frustratingly, though, Mum was determined to satisfy herself that Mrs Oberto really was fit to be out of hospital, and insisted on giving her a thorough check-up in private. Hannah sat in a corner of the corridor outside Mrs Oberto's bedroom for what seemed like hours, until finally Mum came out.

'Okay, you can go in now,' Mum said, smiling. 'But if she starts to get tired – not that it looks likely – you are to come out straight away, and let her rest.'

'Yes, Mum,' said Hannah with a grin, disappearing quickly through Mrs Oberto's door and shutting it behind her.

Chapter 20

Hannah found Mrs Oberto sitting on her bed as usual, her black scarf draped around her shoulders. The old lady patted the bed beside her, and when Hannah sat down next to her, she gave her a huge hug.

'You did it – you helped me.' Mrs Oberto sniffed and blew her nose loudly, as if trying to hide her emotions. 'I saw your card and knew that you had spoken to Tanaquil, and that she must have told you how to help me. When I woke up this morning, it was as though the stroke had never happened.'

Hannah patted the lid of the chest. 'I can't believe it either!' She told Mrs Oberto all about the conversation she'd had with Tanaquil, and the Roman girl's suggestion that Mrs Oberto should sleep under a statue of the god of healing and medicine. Then Hannah explained how she'd decided to try using a picture of the god, instead of a real statue.

'Well done, Hannah!' exclaimed Mrs Oberto, her excitement making her Italian accent sound stronger than ever. 'You believed in me enough to try to contact Tanaquil, even though you must have thought I was mad, and then you were clever enough to think of a way to make Tanaquil's idea work.'

Hannah shook her head slowly. 'I'm finding it hard to believe that a Roman god can really make people better, though, Mrs Oberto, especially in this day and age, with all our modern medicine.' She took the pink ribbon from round her neck, and almost reluctantly gave the key back to Mrs Oberto.

'Well,' answered Mrs Oberto with a smile, taking the key from Hannah and tapping it with her thin finger before hanging it again around her neck, 'maybe we should not try too hard to understand how it worked, but we should just be happy that it did work. At least that is what I am going to do.' She reached into her bag and took out the card with the picture of the Roman god on it. 'I shall always keep this card in my special wooden chest, Hannah. But I hope I am never ill enough to need it again!'

Later on that evening, when Hannah went into her bedroom to get ready for bed, she saw a dirty envelope lying on her pillow. Her heart jumped with delight, and she was just picking it up when Mum walked in, carrying some clean pyjamas.

'Oh, Hannah,' said Mum, her eyes resting on the envelope in Hannah's hand. 'When I took Mrs Oberto her evening drink, she asked me to leave that envelope in your room for you. She said it should be yours now, and to tell you that you never know when you might need it.'

Hannah didn't open the envelope. She didn't need to, to feel the shape of the bronze pendant through the thin paper.

'She wouldn't tell me what was in it, but it's not money, is it?' asked Mum anxiously, flicking her pen nib. 'You know I won't allow you to accept any presents of money from the people who live in the nursing home, don't you?'

'Don't worry, Mum, it's not money. It's just something old that Mrs Oberto thought I might like.' Hannah tried not to show her excitement as she didn't want to arouse Mum's curiosity, and she put the envelope back on her pillow as casually as she could.

Mum fussed about the bedroom, tidying things and putting books back into Hannah's bookcase. Finally, she gave Hannah a kiss goodnight and walked to the door.

'Have a good sleep, Hannah,' she said quietly. 'Don't lie awake for too long. Dad wants you to help him tidy up the rest of the garden after school tomorrow, and you'll need lots of energy for that.'

'Okay, Mum, good night,' Hannah whispered, closing her eyes. She pulled the covers up to her chin and pretended that she was about to fall asleep. As the light went out and the door clicked shut, Hannah's hand closed around the envelope that lay on the pillow next to her head. Was she imagining it, or did it feel slightly warmer than it should? She felt a buzz of excitement as she wondered if or when she might ever see Tanaquil again!

Hannah and Mrs Oberto's adventures will continue soon.

Watch out for further books in the series.

About the Author

Catherine Rosevear lives with her husband, two children and a Tibetan Terrier, in Cambridgeshire, England. She first got the idea for writing the stories about Hannah and Mrs Oberto, when she bought an ancient Roman bronze pendant in the shape of a crescent moon, from an antique dealer. Catherine started to wonder how the pendant had been lost two thousand years ago, what the girl who had been its original owner had been like, and what would happen if she were able to speak to her...

www.catherinerosevear.wordpress.com
Twitter – @cathrosevear
Facebook – @CatherineRosevear2